"Behold, mortals, a beauty that will never fade."

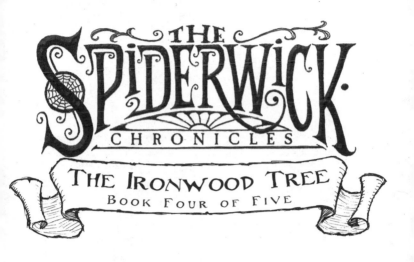

THE SPIDERWICK CHRONICLES

THE IRONWOOD TREE

BOOK FOUR OF FIVE

Tony DiTerlizzi *and* Holly Black

Simon and Schuster Books for Young Readers
New York   London   Toronto   Sydney

SIMON & SCHUSTER BOOKS FOR YOUNG READERS
An imprint of Simon & Schuster Children's Publishing Division
1230 Avenue of the Americas, New York, New York 10020

This jacketed movie tie-in edition January 2008

10   9   8   7   6   5   4   3   2

Library of Congress Cataloging-in-Publication Data
Black, Holly.
The ironwood tree / Holly Black and Tony DiTerlizzi — 1st ed.
p. cm. — (The Spiderwick chronicles ; bk 4)
Summary: After Mallory is kidnapped at her fencing meet, Jared and
Simon search for her near an old quarry and find themselves amidst
dwarves and goblins.
ISBN-13: 978-0-689-85939-7
ISBN-10: 0-689-85939-2
[1. Dwarfs—Fiction. 2. Goblins—Fiction. 3. Brothers and sisters—
Fiction. 4. Twins—Fiction. 5. Caves—Fiction.]
I. DiTerlizzi, Tony. ill. II. Title.
PZ7.B52878Sp 2004
[Fic]—dc22
2004007426

Jacketed edition ISBN-13: 978-1-4169-5020-2
Jacketed edition ISBN-10: 1-4169-5020-6

For my grandmother, Melvina,
who said I should write a book just like this one
and to whom I replied that I never would
—H. B.

For Arthur Rackham,
may you continue to inspire others
as you have me
—T. D.

Table of Contents

List of Full-Page Illustrations

Dear Reader,

Over the years that Tony and I have been friends, we've shared the same childhood fascination with faeries. We did not realize the importance of that bond or how it might be tested.

One day Tony and I—along with several other authors—were doing a signing at a large bookstore. When the signing was over, we lingered, helping to stack books and chatting, until a clerk approached us. He said that there had been a letter left for us. When I inquired which one of us, we were surprised by his answer.

"Both of you," he said.

The letter was exactly as reproduced on the following page. Tony spent a long time just staring at the photocopy that came with it. Then, in a hushed voice, he wondered aloud about the remainder of the manuscript. We hurriedly wrote a note, tucked it back into the envelope, and asked the clerk to deliver it to the Grace children.

Not long after, a package arrived on my doorstep, bound in red ribbon. A few days after that, three children rang the bell and told me this story.

What has happened since is hard to describe. Tony and I have been plunged into a world we never quite believed in. We now see that faeries are far more than childhood stories. There is an invisible world around us and we hope that you, dear reader, will open your eyes to it.

HOLLY BLACK

Dear Mrs. Black and Mr. DiTerlizzi:

I know that a lot of people don't believe in faeries, but I do and I think that you do too. After I read your books, I told my brothers about you and we decided to write. We know about real faeries. In fact, we know a lot about them.

The page attached* to this one is a photocopy from an old book we found in our attic. It isn't a great copy because we had some trouble with the copier. The book tells people how to identify faeries and how to protect themselves. Can you please give this book to your publisher? If you can, please put a letter in this envelope and give it back to the store. We will find a way to send the book. The normal mail is too dangerous.

We just want people to know about this. The stuff that has happened to us could happen to anyone.

Sincerely,

Mallory, Jared, and Simon Grace

*Not included.

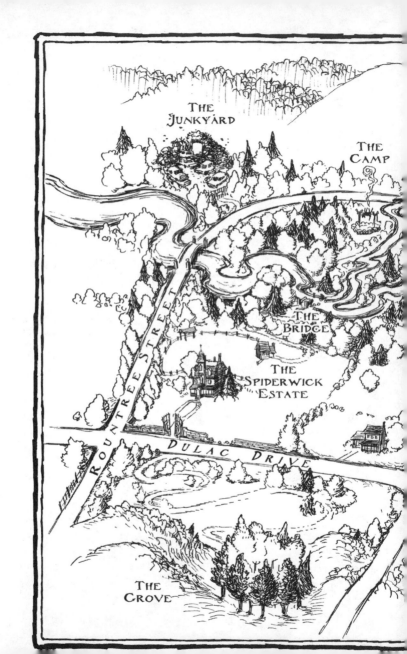

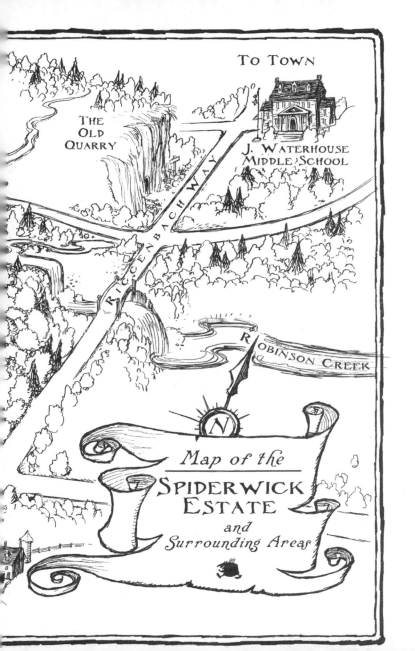

"It's an abandoned quarry."

Chapter One

IN WHICH There Is Both a Fight and a Duel

The engine of the station wagon was already running. Mallory leaned against the door, her everyday sneakers grungy against the bright white of her long fencing socks. Her hair was gelled and pulled back into a ponytail so tight that it made her eyes bulge. Mrs. Grace stood on the driver's side, her hands on her hips.

"I found him!" Jared panted, running up to join them.

"Simon," their mother called. "Where were you? We looked everywhere!"

"The carriage house," Simon said. "Taking care of the . . . uh, a bird I found." Simon looked uncomfortable. He wasn't used to having to lie. That was mostly Jared's job.

Mallory rolled her eyes. "Too bad Mom wouldn't leave without you."

"Mallory," their mother said, shaking her head in disapproval. "All of you—get in the car. We're going to be late already, and I still have to drop something off."

As Mallory turned to put her bag in the trunk, Jared noticed that her chest looked strange. Stiff and weirdly . . . big.

"What are you wearing?" he asked, pointing.

"Shut up," she said.

He snickered. "It's just that you look like you've got—"

"Shut up!" she said again, getting into the front seat of the car while the boys climbed in the back. "It's for protection, and I have to have it on."

Jared smiled against the window and watched the woods go by. There hadn't been any faerie activity in more than two weeks—even Thimbletack had been quiet—and occasionally Jared had to remind himself that it was real. Sometimes it seemed like everything could be explained away. Even the burning water had been dismissed as simply being from a contaminated well. Until the old plumbing could be connected to a central line, they used gallons of supermarket water without Mom thinking it was strange. But there was Simon's griffin, and *that* couldn't be explained by anything but Arthur's field guide.

"Stop chewing on your ponytail," their mother said to Mallory. "What is making you so jittery? Is this new team really that good?"

"I'm fine," Mallory said.

Back in New York she'd fenced in sweat-pants and a team jacket chosen from a pile. There had been a guy who'd hold up his hand on your side if you had scored. But at the new school, fencers wore real uniforms and had elec-tric rapiers wired to a scoring machine that flashed lights when someone got hit. Jared thought that was enough to make anyone jumpy.

Apparently their mother had another explanation. "It's that boy, isn't it? The one

4

you were talking to on Wednesday when I picked you up."

"What boy?" Simon asked from the backseat, already starting to laugh.

"Be quiet," said their mother, but she answered anyway. "Chris, the fencing captain. He is the captain, isn't he?"

Their sister grunted noncommittally.

"Chris and Mallory sitting in a tree, K-I-S-S-I-N G," Simon sang. Jared giggled, and Mallory turned toward the backseat, eyes narrowed.

"Want to lose all your baby teeth at once?"

"Don't listen to them," their mother said. "And *don't* worry. You're a smart, pretty girl and a great fencer. I bet he likes you."

"*Mom!*" Mallory groaned and sank lower in the front seat.

Their mother stopped at the library where she worked, dropped off some paperwork, and

"I bet he likes you."

returned to the idling car, somewhat out of breath.

"Come on! I can't be late," Mallory said, smoothing her hair back unnecessarily. "It's my first match!"

Their mother sighed. "We're almost there."

Jared resumed looking out the window in time to see what looked like a deep crater. They were driving over a stone bridge. The school bus never went this way.

"Simon, look! What's that?"

"It's an abandoned quarry," Mallory said impatiently. "Where people used to dig up rocks."

"A *quarry*," Jared echoed. He remembered something from the map they'd found in their great-uncle Arthur's study.

"Think they found any fossils?" Simon asked, half crawling over Jared to look out the

window. "I wonder what dinosaurs lived in this area."

Their mother was already pulling the car into the school parking lot. She didn't answer.

Jared, Simon, and their mother climbed up onto the gymnasium bleachers while Mallory went to sit with her team. Already seated were a few other families and a smattering of people Jared recognized from school. A rectangular pad was spread out on the floor with lines taped on it. Mallory called it a *piste,* but Jared thought it just looked like a long, black mat. Behind it was a folding table where the scoreboard sat, its large, colored buttons making it look more like a game than something important. The director was fiddling with the wires, connecting them to a foil and testing the force needed to make the buzzer sound and the lights flash.

Mallory sat down on a metal chair at one

end of the *piste* and started unpacking her bag. Chris squatted down to talk with Mallory. The other team milled around the opposite end. All the uniforms were so white, they made Jared's eyes hurt.

Finally the director announced it was time for the first bout. He called two fencers up and made each of them strap a small receiver to the back of their pants, then attached cords to their foils. It all looked so professional. As the fencers began, Jared tried to recall what Mallory had said about the flashing lights, but he couldn't.

"This is stupid. I like fencing better without all this junk," Jared said to no one in particular.

Two matches later Jared had figured out that the colored lights meant that the hit was good, but the white light meant that the hit didn't count. Only hits in the chest counted. Which was dumb, really, Jared had always thought. Getting hit in the leg hurt plenty, and Jared had practiced with Mallory enough to know.

Finally Mallory was called to the mat. Her opponent—a tall boy called Daniel Something-or-Other—snickered as he put on his mask. He obviously had no idea what was coming.

Jared elbowed Simon as his brother put a pretzel into his mouth. "He's going to get it."

"Ow," said Simon. "Cut it out."

Mallory's ponytail bounced as she advanced. Her sword struck Daniel hard in the chest before he could parry. The director raised one hand, and the scoreboard lit up with a point for Mallory. Jared grinned.

Their mother was craning her whole body forward as if there were something to hear other than the clang of thin metal blades locked

"I like fencing better without all this junk."

in the pattern of attack, parry, and riposte. Daniel lunged desperately, too upset to control his advance. Mallory countered, turning her defense into an attack and scoring another point.

Their sister beat Daniel without being touched once. They saluted each other formally, and the boy took off his mask, red-faced and breathing hard. When Mallory's mask came off, she smiled, eyes slitted with satisfaction.

On the way back to the metal chairs the fencing captain gave Mallory a quick awkward hug. Jared couldn't see very well, but he could have sworn that Mallory's face flushed darker than it had been when she stepped off the mat.

The bouts went on, with Mallory's team doing pretty well. When it was the captain's turn to fence, Mallory cheered loudly. Unfortunately it didn't seem to help. He was defeated by a narrow margin. Slinking back to his seat, he walked past her without a word and shrugged off her attempts to talk to him.

When Mallory was called to the mat again, Chris didn't even look up.

Jared watched from the stands and scowled. His scowl deepened when he noticed a blond-haired girl in white fencing garb rooting through his sister's bag.

"Who's that?" Jared pointed.

Simon shrugged. "I dunno. She hasn't fenced yet."

Could the girl be a friend of his sister? Maybe she was just borrowing something? The furtive way the girl stopped when anyone from the team looked her way made Jared think she was stealing. But what would anyone want in a bag of Mallory's dirty socks and spare foils?

Clang of thin metal blades

Jared stood up. He had to do something. Didn't anyone else notice what was happening?

"Where are you going?" his mother asked.

"Bathroom," he lied automatically, even though his mother would be able to see him walking across the gym. He wished he could tell her the truth, but she would have made up some excuse for the girl. She thought the best of everyone, except him.

Jared climbed down the bleachers and, staying close to the wall, crossed the court to where the girl was still rummaging. But as Jared approached the chairs, the coach stopped him.

The fencing coach was wiry and short, with patchy white stubble on his face. "Sorry, kid, you can't come over here during the meet."

The coach stopped him.

"But that girl's trying to steal my sister's stuff!"

The coach turned. "Who?"

As Jared swung around to point her out, though, he realized that she'd disappeared. He fumbled for an explanation. "I don't know who she is. She hasn't fenced yet."

"Everybody's fenced, kid. I think you'd better go back to your seat."

Jared turned back to the bleachers, embarrassed, then thought better of it. He'd go out to the bathroom so that maybe his mother would ask fewer questions when he returned. Just before he walked through the blue gym doors, he stopped and looked back. Now *Simon* was fumbling through Mallory's bag. But Simon was wearing *his* clothes! Everyone would think it was him. He narrowed his eyes, wishing what he saw made sense.

Then a horrible suspicion formed in his mind. Glancing up into the stands, he caught sight of his brother sitting beside his mother, chewing on pretzels. Whatever that thing was, it wasn't Simon.

"Don't you know me?"

Chapter Two

IN WHICH the Grace Twins Are Triplets

Jared couldn't move from the doorway. He heard the clanging of swords and cheering, but the sounds seemed to come from far away. He watched in horror as the coach confronted his double. The man got red in the face, and some of the other players looked at Jared's double in shock.

"Great." Jared grimaced. There was no way he could explain this.

The coach pointed toward the large gym door, and he watched Not-Jared stalk toward it—and toward him. As Not-Jared got closer to Jared, it smirked. Jared clenched his hands into fists.

Not-Jared passed Jared without a single glance, slamming through the double doors. Jared wanted to find some way to wipe that smile off its face. He followed after it, into a hallway lined with lockers.

"Who are you?" Jared demanded. "What do you want?"

Not-Jared turned to face him, and something in its eyes made Jared go cold all over. "Don't you know me? Am I not your own self?" Its mouth curled into a sneer.

It was strange to watch it move and speak. It wasn't like watching Simon, with his tidy hair and the smear of toothpaste on his upper lip. And it wasn't quite himself either—the hair was messier, and the eyes were darker and . . .

different. It took a step toward
him.

Jared took a step
back, wishing for any
kind of faerie protec-
tion, and then he
remembered the
pocketknife in his
jeans. Faeries hated
iron, and steel was
at least part iron. He
opened one of the
blades. "Why don't you
all just leave us alone?"

THE
NOT-JARED

The creature threw back
its head and laughed. "You can never
get away from your own self."

"Shut up! You're not me." Jared pointed
the knife at his double.

"Put that toy away," Not-Jared said, its voice low and harsh.

"I don't know who you are, or who sent you, but bet I know what you're looking for," said Jared. "The Guide. Well, you're never going to get it."

The creature's grin widened into something that still wasn't really a smile. Then suddenly it shrank back as though frightened. Jared watched in amazement as the Not-Jared's body shrank, its dark hair paled into a sandy brown, and its now blue eyes went wide with terror.

Before Jared could fully comprehend what he was seeing, he heard a woman's voice behind him.

"What's going on here? Put that knife down."

The vice principal rushed up, grabbing Jared's wrist. The pocketknife clattered to the linoleum floor. Jared stared at the blade as the sandy-haired boy ran off down the hall, his sobs sounding a lot like laughter.

"I can't believe you brought your knife to school," Simon whispered to Jared as they sat together outside the vice principal's office.

Jared shot him a look. He had explained several times — even once to the police — that he was only *showing* the kid the knife, but they'd never found the other boy to confirm the story. Then the vice principal had asked Jared to wait outside. Their mother had been in the vice principal's office a long time, but Jared couldn't hear what was going on.

"What kind of faerie do you think that thing was?" Simon asked.

"What kind of faerie do you think it was?"

Jared shrugged. "I wish we had the book so I could look it up."

"You don't remember anything that could shape-shift like that?"

"I don't know." Jared rubbed his face.

"Look, I told Mom it wasn't your fault. You'll just have to explain."

Jared gave a short laugh. "Yeah, like I can tell her what happened."

"I could say that kid stole something from Mallory's bag." When Jared didn't respond, Simon tried again. "I could pretend I did it. We could switch shirts and everything."

Jared just shook his head.

Finally their mother emerged from the vice principal's office. She looked tired.

"I'm sorry," Jared said.

He was surprised by the calm tone of her voice. "I don't want to talk about it, Jared.

Get your sister and let's just go."

Jared nodded and followed Simon, looking back just in time to see their mother sink down in the chair he'd vacated. What was she thinking? Why wasn't she yelling? He found himself wishing that she was mad—at least *that* he would understand. Her quiet sadness was more frightening. It was like this was all she *expected* of him.

Simon and Jared walked through the school, stopping to ask fencing team members if they'd seen Mallory. None of them had. They even stopped Chris-the-captain. He looked uncomfortable when they asked about Mallory, but he shook his head. The gymnasium was empty, the only sounds the echo of their steps on the glossy wood floor. The black mat had been rolled up, and everything from the meet had been put away.

Finally a girl with long, brown hair told them she'd seen Mallory crying in the girls' bathroom.

Simon shook his head. "Mallory? Crying? But she won."

The girl shrugged. "I asked her if she was okay, but she said she was fine."

"You think that was really her?" Simon asked as they walked toward the restroom.

"You mean, was something impersonating her? Why would a faerie turn into Mallory and then cry in a girls' bathroom?"

"I don't know," said Simon. "I'd cry if I had to turn into Mallory."

Jared snorted. "So, you want to go in there and look for her?"

"I'm not going into the girls' room," Simon said. "Besides, you're already in so much trouble, there's no way you can get into more."

"I can *always* get into more trouble," Jared said with a sigh. He pushed open the door. It looked surprisingly like the boys' room, except there were no urinals.

"Mallory?" he called. No answer. He peered under the stalls but didn't see any feet. He pushed open one of the doors gingerly. Even though there was no one in there, he felt weird, jumpy and embarrassed. After a moment he darted back out into the hall.

"She's not in there?" Simon said.

"It's empty." Jared glanced past the line of lockers, hoping no one had seen him.

"Maybe she went to the office looking for us," Simon said. "I don't see her anywhere."

A feeling of dread uncoiled in the pit of Jared's stomach. After the vice principal had caught him, he hadn't really thought about anything but how much trouble he was in. But

"Mallory?"

that thing was still running around the school. He remembered how the creature had looked through Mallory's bag at the match.

"What if she went outside?" Jared said, hoping that they could still find her before it did. "She could have gone out to see if we were waiting by the car."

"We could look." Simon shrugged. Jared could tell he wasn't convinced, but they walked outside anyway.

The sky had already deepened to purples and golds. In the dimming light they walked past the track and the baseball field.

"I don't see her," Simon said.

Jared nodded. His stomach churned with nervousness. *Where is she?* he wondered.

"Hey," Simon said. "What's that?" He walked a few feet and leaned down to pick up something shining in the grass.

"Mallory's fencing medal," Jared said. "And look."

On the grass large chunks of rock formed a circle around the medal. Jared knelt down beside the largest stone. Engraved deeply in the rock was a word: TRADE.

"Stones," Simon said. "Like from the quarry."

Jared looked up, surprised. "Remember the map we found? It said dwarves live in the quarry—but I don't think dwarves can shape-shift."

"Mallory could still be inside with Mom. She could be in the office waiting for us."

Jared wanted to believe it. "Then why is her medal out here?"

"Maybe she dropped it. Maybe this is a trap." Simon started walking back toward the school. "Come on," he said. "Let's go back and see if she's with Mom."

Jared nodded numbly.

When they got back inside, they found their mother in the school entrance, talking into her cell phone. Her back was to them, and she was alone.

Although their mother was speaking softly, her voice traveled easily to where they crouched. "Yeah, I thought things were getting better too. But, you know, Jared never admitted to what happened when we first moved here . . . and well, this is going to sound strange, but Mallory and Simon are so protective of him."

Jared froze, both dreading what she was going to say and unable to make himself do anything to stop her from continuing.

"No, no. They deny he ever did any of those things. And they're keeping something from me. I can tell by the way they stop talking when they come into a room, the way they cover for one another, especially for Jared. You should have heard Simon tonight, making up excuses for his brother pulling a knife on that little boy." Here she made a choked noise and began crying.

"I just don't know if I can handle him anymore. He is so angry, Richard. Maybe he should go and stay with you for a while."

Jared froze.

Dad. She was talking to their dad.

Simon jabbed Jared in the arm. "Come on. Mallory's not here."

Jared turned dazedly and followed his brother out the door. He could not have said how he felt at that moment — except maybe hollow.

SEEM TO TRICK HEN TOOK PEN

Chapter Three

IN WHICH Simon Solves a Riddle

W hat are we going to do?" Simon asked as they walked back down the hallway.

"They have her," Jared said softly. He had to blot out what he'd just heard, blot everything from his mind except Mallory. "They want to trade her for the Guide."

"But we don't have it."

"Shhh!" Jared said. He had an idea, but he didn't want to say it aloud, out in the open air. "Come on."

Jared went to his locker and got a towel

from his gym bag. He picked out a textbook — *Advanced Mathematics* — that was about the same size as the Guide and folded it in the cloth.

"What are you doing?"

"Here," he whispered, shoving the wrapped package at Simon. He grabbed his backpack from the locker. "Thimbletack fooled us with this trick. Maybe we can fool whoever took Mallory."

Simon nodded once. "Okay, I think Mom has a flashlight in the car."

They clambered over a chain-link fence at the edge of the schoolyard and crossed the highway. The other side of the road was overgrown with weeds. It was hard to walk in the dark, and the flashlight gave off only a faint narrow light.

They climbed over a large pile of rocks, some covered in slick moss, others cracked in parts. As they went, Jared couldn't stop replaying what he'd overheard. He thought about the awful things that his mother believed and the even more-awful things she was likely to believe now that he'd disappeared. No matter what he did, he wound up in deeper and deeper trouble. What if he were expelled? What if she were to send him out to live with his dad, who wouldn't want him?

"Jared, look," said Simon. They had come to the edge of the old quarry.

The rock had been mined jaggedly; chunks of stone stuck out like ledges along the nearly thirty-foot drop to the uneven valley below. Scrubby bits of grass grew along the walls from thick veins of dirt. The highway ran over the top of the cavern, elevated on a thick stone bridge.

"It's weird to mine rocks, isn't it?" Simon asked. "I mean, they're just *rocks*.

"Probably granite," he continued when Jared didn't answer. Simon wrapped his thin jacket tighter around himself.

Jared shone his flashlight along the walls, catching a streak of rust and a blush of ochre in the beam. He had no idea what kind of stone it was.

Simon shrugged. "So, uh, how are we going to get down there?"

"I don't know. Why don't you tell me, if you know so much?" Jared snapped.

"We could . . . ," Simon started, but he trailed off and Jared felt bad.

"Let's just try to climb down," said Jared, pointing. "We can jump to that ledge and then try to get to another one."

"That's pretty far down. We should get a rope or something."

"That's pretty far down."

"We don't have time," Jared said. "Here, hold the light."

Thrusting the metal cylinder into his twin's hands, Jared sat on the edge of the cliff. Without the flashlight, when he looked down, he saw only the deep darkness below. Taking a breath, he scooted off, letting himself drop to a stone shelf he could not see.

Turning, he started to stand. Light shone in his eyes, blinding him. He stumbled and fell forward.

"Are you all right?" Simon called.

Jared shaded his face and tried to keep calm. "Yeah. Come on. Your turn."

He heard the crunching of dirt above him as Simon got into position. Quickly Jared moved out of the way, feeling ahead of him for an edge he only dimly remembered. Simon landed heavily beside him with a yelp.

The flashlight tumbled from Simon's hands

and fell into the darkness, hitting the valley floor hard, bouncing once and then lying still, illuminating a thin path of scrub and stone.

"How could you be so dumb!" Jared felt his temper like it was a living thing inside him, growing by the minute. Only shouting seemed to keep it from overwhelming him. "Why didn't you throw

45

it down to me? How are we going to climb down in the dark? What if Mallory's in danger? What if she *dies* because you were such a moron?"

Simon's head came up, his eyes shining with tears, but Jared was as shocked as his brother.

"I didn't mean it, Simon," he said hastily.

Simon nodded, but turned his face away from Jared.

"I think there's another ledge there. See that shape?"

Simon still didn't say anything.

"I'll go first," Jared said. He took a deep breath and dropped into the blackness. He hit the second ledge hard—it must have been farther down than he'd thought. His breath was knocked out of him, and his hands and knees were on fire. Slowly he pushed himself upright. His jeans were ripped widely over one knee, and his arm had a cut that started to bleed sluggishly. But from there it was only a short hop down to the quarry floor.

"Jared?" Simon's voice came faintly from where he was still sitting on the top ledge.

"I'm here," Jared called. "Don't move. I'll get the light."

He crawled over to grab the flashlight and turned it toward his brother, searching out ledges where Simon could step or niches he could grab. Slowly Simon climbed his way to the ground. But as he waited, Jared noticed echoing sounds, a distant thrum and a pounding that seemed to come from nowhere and everywhere at once.

Shining the flashlight around the quarry, he saw more jagged rock with faint traces of drill lines. He now wondered how they were ever going to get out. But before he had time to worry about that, the light flashed on an overhang of rock on the wall. As the light passed over the stone, a mottled pattern of fungi gave off a dim bluish glow.

"Bioluminescence," Simon said.

"Huh?" Jared took a step closer.

"When something makes its own light."

By the weak glow, Jared saw that a rectangle of stone under the ledge had been carved with a pattern of intertwining grooves. Looking at the center of the rock, he could make out the tops of letters hewn into the stone. He turned the flashlight directly on them.

SEEM TO TRICK HEN TOOK PEN

"A riddle," said Jared.

"It doesn't make any sense," said Simon.

"Who cares about that? How do we solve it?" They didn't have time to stand around now. They were almost inside, almost to Mallory.

"You solved the one back at the house," said Simon, sitting down with his back to his brother. "You figure it out."

Jared took a deep breath. "Look, I'm really sorry about what I said before. You have to help," Jared pleaded. "Everyone knows you're smarter than I am."

Simon sighed. "I don't understand the riddle either. A hen is a girl chicken, right? And a pen could be the place where they keep chickens. I don't know about the rest."

Jared looked at the words again. He couldn't seem to concentrate. What trick could a chicken perform? Maybe they were supposed to offer eggs at the entrance? Did the Guide say anything about chickens and faeries? He wished he had the book now. . . .

"Hey, wait a minute," Simon said, turning around and kneeling up. "Give me that light."

Jared handed over the flashlight and watched as Simon scratched out the message in the thin dirt with his finger. Then he started scratching out certain letters and writing them above in a different pattern.

MITES OPEN THREE TOCK KON

"What are you doing?" Jared sat down beside his twin.

50

J. WATERHOUSE MIDDLE SCHOOL

DATE: _October 11_

STUDENT NAME: __Grace, Jared__

SEX:_M_ GRADE:_4_ AGE:_9_ SSN:_134-00-2067_

STUDENT LIVES WITH: _x_ Mother ___Father ___Both ___Other

___Jared Grace___ HAS BEEN SUSPENDED FROM J. WATERHOUSE MIDDLE

SCHOOL FOR A PERIOD OF __10__ DAYS.

DURING THIS TIME, THE STUDENT IS BANNED FROM CAMPUS AND ALL SCHOOL FUNCTIONS. THIS IS THE STUDENT'S _first_ SUSPENSION AND IS FOR THE FOLLOWING REASONS:
On October the eleventh, Jared Grace was seen in the hallway during an athletic event, threatening another child with a knife. In accordance with our policy, any student who is found on school premises, at school-sponsored or school-related events, in possession of a dangerous weapon (see chapter 55C for what constitutes a dangerous weapon under the school guidelines) or controlled substance may be subject to expulsion from the school or school district.

WE REGRET THAT IT IS NECESSARY TO TAKE THIS DISCIPLINARY ACTION. IF YOU DESIRE FURTHER INFORMATION ON THIS MATTER, YOU MAY CONTACT ME DIRECTLY AT THE SCHOOL.

GRADED SCHOOLWORK MISSED BY A STUDENT ON AN OUT-OF-SCHOOL SUSPENSION CANNOT BE MADE UP.

WE ARE HOPEFUL OUR COORDINATED EFFORTS WILL LEAD TO A BETTER UNDERSTANDING AND SOLUTION TO THE PROBLEM.

COMMENTS:
Due to previous disciplinary problems in the classroom here and at his previous school as well as the serious nature of this incident, expulsion is recommended. A hearing before the school board will be scheduled. You and your son are encouraged to attend and present any information you feel will be material to a decision on this matter.

THE ABOVE NAMED STUDENT HAS BEEN AFFORDED DUE PROCESS AND ALL SUSPENSION/EXPULSION PROCEDURES HAVE BEEN FOLLOWED AS DIRECTED BY STATE LAW.

PRINCIPAL'S SIGNATURE_____

Carbon copy of Jared Grace's expulsion letter.

"I think you have to rearrange the letters to get the real message. Like those puzzles in the paper that Mom is always doing." Simon inscribed a third phrase in the dust.

KNOCK THREE TIMES TO OPEN

"Wow," said Jared. He couldn't believe that Simon had figured it out. He never would have solved it.

Simon grinned. "Easy," he said, walking up to the door and knocking three times on the hard stone face.

Just then the ground shifted underneath them, and both twins fell into the chasm that opened beneath their feet.

"What have we here? Prisoners!"

Chapter Four

IN WHICH the Twins Discover a Tree Unlike Any Other

They tumbled down into a net of woven metal. Yelping and kicking, Jared tried to stand, but he couldn't seem to get a foothold. Abruptly he stopped struggling and got elbowed in the ear by his brother.

"Simon, stop! Look!"

Glowing fungi covered the walls in patches, illuminating the faces of three small men with skin as gray as stone. Their clothes were drab and sewn from rough fabrics, but their silver bracelets, crafted in the shape of serpents, were so intricate that they seemed to slither around the men's thin arms; their collars were woven with golden threads beaten so fine that they might have been cloth; and their jeweled rings were so lovely that each of their dirty fingers gleamed.

"What have we here? Prisoners!" said one with a voice like gravel. "Seldom have we any live prisoners."

"Dwarves," Jared whispered to his brother.

"They don't seem very 'hi-ho, hi-ho,'" Simon whispered back.

The second dwarf rubbed several strands of Jared's hair between his fingers and turned to the one who had spoken. "Not very extraordinary, are they? The black of their tresses is dull and plain. Their skin is neither smooth nor pale as marble. I find them ill made. We could do far better."

Jared scowled, not sure what the dwarf meant. Again, he wished for the Guide. He remembered only that dwarves were great craftspeople, and the iron that hurt other faeries didn't bother them. His knife would have been useless, even if it hadn't been confiscated.

THE KORTING

"We're here for our sister," Jared said. "We want to trade."

One of them chuckled, but Jared wasn't sure which. With a creak another dwarf positioned a silvery cage beneath the netting.

"The Korting said you would come. He is very eager to meet you."

"Is he like the dwarf king or something?" Simon asked.

The dwarves did not answer. One pulled on a carved handle and the net opened. Both boys fell heavily into the cage. Jared's hands and knees felt raw all over again. He slammed his fist against the metal floor.

Jared and Simon were silent as they were wheeled through caverns with cold air and wet walls. They could hear the sounds of hammers, louder and more distinct now that they were underground, and the roaring of what might have been a great fire. Overhead in the gloom, patches of dim phosphorescence showed the tips of large stalactites, hanging above them like a forest of icicles.

They passed through a grotto where bats shrieked from above, and the floor was dark and rank with their droppings. Jared tried to contain a shiver. The deeper they went, the colder the cavern became. Sometimes Jared saw shadows shift in the gloom and heard an erratic tapping.

As they moved through a narrow corridor, past dripping columns, Jared breathed in the damp, mineral scent with relief after the stink of the bats. The next chamber seemed to be filled with dusty piles of metal objects. A golden rat with sapphire eyes darted out of a malachite goblet and watched them pass. A silver rabbit lay on its side, a winding key around its neck, while a single bud of a platinum lily opened, then closed, then opened again. Simon looked at the metal rat with longing.

Then they moved into a large cavern where they saw dwarves carving statues of other dwarves into the granite walls. The sudden brightness of the lantern light stung Jared's eyes, but as he passed the dwarves, he thought he saw one of the carving's arms move.

From there they moved into an enormous space where a massive tree grew underground. The thick trunk reached up until it was lost in the shadows, branches forming a canopy over them. The air was filled with a strange metallic birdsong.

"That can't be a tree," Simon said. "There's no sun. No sun means no photosynthesis."

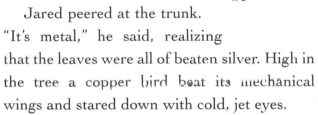

Jared peered at the trunk. "It's metal," he said, realizing that the leaves were all of beaten silver. High in the tree a copper bird beat its mechanical wings and stared down with cold, jet eyes.

"The first ironwood tree," said one of the dwarves. "Behold, mortals, a beauty that will never fade."

Jared looked up at the tree with awe, amazed by how one metal had been forged as rough as bark and twisted into branches while another was as delicate as filigree. Each silver leaf was unique, veined and curled like a real one.

"Behold, mortals, a beauty that will never fade."

"Why do you call us mortals?" Jared asked.

"Don't you know your own tongue?" a dwarf said, and snorted. "It means one who is fated for death. What else should we call you? Your kind wither in a blink of the eye." He leaned close to the bars of the cage and winked.

Several passages led from the cavern out into corridors that were too dim for Jared to see where they led. The cage was wheeled through one—a wide, columned hallway that led into a smaller room. Sitting on a throne hewn from an enormous stalagmite was another gray-skinned man, this one with a wiry black beard. His eyes shone like green jewels. A metal dog stretched out on a deerskin rug before the throne, the dog's side rising and falling in time with a thin mechanical wheeze, just as if it were really sleeping. On its back a single key slowly turned.

"My lord Korting."

Around the throne were other dwarves, all of them silent.

"My lord Korting," said one of the dwarves. "It is as you said. They have come looking for their sister."

The Korting stood. "Mulgarath told me you would come. How fortunate you are to be here, how honored that you will see the beginning of the end of human rule."

"Whatever," Jared said. "Where's Mallory?"

The Korting scowled. "Bring her," he said, and several of the dwarves immediately shuffled off. "You would do well to watch what you say. Mulgarath will soon reign over the world, and we, his loyal servants, will be at his side. He will strip the land bare for us and then we will build a glorious new forest of ironwood trees. We will rebuild the world in silver and copper and iron."

Simon crawled to the edge of the cage.

"That doesn't make any sense. What are you going to eat? How are you going to breathe without plants to make oxygen?"

Jared smiled at Simon. Sometimes it wasn't so bad having a know-it-all for a twin brother.

The Korting's scowl deepened. "Do you deny that we dwarves are the greatest crafts-people you have ever seen? You need only to look at my hound there to see our superiority. His silver body is more lovely than any fur, he is faster, he needs no food, and he neither drools nor fawns." The Korting nudged the dog with his foot. The dog turned and stretched before resuming its wheezy sleep.

"I don't think that's what Simon was trying to say," Jared began, but he was interrupted by six dwarves entering the room, a long glass box on their shoulders.

"Mallory!" Jared stared with a sinking feeling in his stomach. The case looked like a coffin.

"What did you do to our sister?" Simon demanded. He looked pale. "She's not dead, is she?"

"Just the opposite," said the dwarf lord with a smile. "She will never die. Look more closely."

The dwarves set down the glass case on an ornately sculpted stand beside Jared and Simon's cage.

Mallory's hair had been arranged and hung in one long braid snaking past her waxy, pale face. A circlet of metal leaves rested above her forehead. Her lips and cheeks were rouged as red as a doll's, yet her hands held the hilt of a silvery blade.

She had been dressed in a white gown of frothy lace. Her eyes were closed, and Jared was almost afraid that if she opened them, they would be made of glass.

"What did they do to her?" said Simon. "It doesn't seem like Mallory at all."

"Her beauty and youth will never fade," said the Korting. "Out of this case she would be doomed to age, death, and decay—the curse of all mortals."

"I think Mallory would rather be doomed," said Jared.

The dwarf lord snorted. "Suit yourself. What have you to give me for her?"

Jared reached into his backpack and brought out the towel-wrapped book. "Arthur Spiderwick's field guide." He felt a twinge of guilt at the lie but ruthlessly quashed it.

The Korting rubbed his hands together. "Excellent. Just as was anticipated. Let's have the book."

"You'll give my sister back to me?"

"She'll be yours."

Jared held out the fake field guide, and one of the dwarves snatched it through the bars. The dwarf lord did not even bother to look at it.

"Take this fine cage to the treasure room, and put the glass case beside it!"

"What?" Jared said. "But you wanted to trade!'"

"We *have* traded," the Korting said with a sneer. "You bargained for your sister, but you never bargained for your freedom."

"No! You can't!" Jared banged his hands on the bars, but it did not keep the dwarves from pushing their moving prison out into a dark corridor. He couldn't look at Simon. After all his yelling at his brother, it was he who was the stupid one, he who hadn't been clever enough. He felt tired and worn-out, small and pathetic. He was just a kid. How was he supposed to find a way out of this?

"You're going to have to feed us."

Chapter Five

IN WHICH Jared and Simon Wake Sleeping Beauty

Jared barely noticed the path they took to the treasure room. He shut his eyes against the burn of tears.

"Here we are," said the dwarf who had brought them. His beard was white, and there was a ring of keys at his hip. He turned to the group carrying the glass box that held Mallory. "Just set that down right there."

The treasure chamber was lit with a single lantern, but the heaps of shining gold reflected the light, so it was not as dim as it might have been. A silver peacock with a lapis-and-coral-studded tail pecked at a copper mouse sitting atop a vase in a way that suggested more boredom than malice.

The white-bearded dwarf peered at them while the others trooped out. He grinned at them fondly. "I'll just see if I can find something for you boys to play with. Perhaps gob stones? They even stand up and hurl themselves."

"I'm hungry," Simon said. "We're not mechanical. If you're going to keep us here, you're going to have to feed us."

The dwarf squinted. "True enough. I'll bring you a mash of spiders and turnips. That will fix you right up."

"How are you going to give it to us?" Jared asked suddenly. "There's no door."

"Oh, there's a door all right," said the dwarf. "I made that cage myself. Sturdy, isn't it?"

"Yeah," said Jared. "Real sturdy." He rolled his eyes. Wasn't it bad enough that they had gotten tricked and were stuck in a *cage*? Did the dwarf really have to rub it in?

"See, the lock is inside this bar." The dwarf tapped one of the bars lightly with his finger. "I had to make the gears really tiny— had to work with a hammer the size of a pin.

If you look, you can see the seam of the door. See? Right there."

"Can you open it?" Simon asked. Jared looked at him with surprise. Had Simon been planning the whole time, while Jared had been busy just being upset?

"You want to see it in action?" asked the dwarf.

"Yeah," Jared said, not quite believing that they were going to get this lucky.

"Well, okay, boys. Now step back for a moment. There. Just once, and then I better get your food. What a treat to finally get to use all of these things."

Jared smiled encouragingly. The dwarf took the key ring from his belt and selected a tiny key. It was the size and shape of a whistle, with a complicated pattern of ridges on it. He inserted it into one of the bars, although Jared couldn't see the hole from their side of the cage. With a twist of the dwarf's wrist, clicks, clunks, whirrs, and whizzing noises came from the whole rail.

"There." The dwarf pulled on the bar, and a front section of the cage swung open on hidden hinges. But just as the boys were moving forward, the dwarf quickly shut it. "Wouldn't have been as much fun if you hadn't at least tried to escape," he chuckled, moving to hook the key ring back on his belt.

Jared darted his hand out and grabbed for the key ring at the same time. The keys clattered to the floor.

Simon scooped them up before the dwarf could.

"Hey! No fair!" said the dwarf. "Give those back!"

Simon shook his head.

"But you have to. You're prisoners. You can't have the keys."

"We're not giving them back," Jared said.

The dwarf looked panicked. He walked to the edge of the hall and yelled, "Quick— someone! Send guards! The prisoners are escaping!" When no one came, he fixed Jared and Simon with a glare. "You'd better stay right there," he said, and darted out into the hall, still calling for guards.

Simon fitted the key into the door, and they jumped out of the cage. "Hurry, they're coming!"

"We have to get Mallory!" Jared gestured to her case.

"There's no time," said Simon. "We'll come back."

"Wait," Jared said. "Let's hide here! They'll think we ran away."

Simon looked panicked. "Where?"

"On top of the cage!" Jared pointed to the solid silver lid of the cage. He scrambled on top of a nearby pile of loot and used it to climb up. "Come on!"

Simon climbed halfway, and Jared hauled him onto the top. They had just enough time to curl up tightly before dwarves burst into the room.

"They're not here, either," one dwarf said. "Not in the hallway, not in any of the nearby rooms."

Jared smirked against the cool metal.

"Wind up the dogs. They'll find them."

"Dogs?" Simon mouthed to Jared as the dwarves shuffled out of the room.

"What's the matter?" Jared smiled, giddy at the success of their plan. "You love dogs."

Simon rolled his eyes and dropped to the

"They're not here, either."

floor, kicking a candelabrum and scattering a few pieces of hematite. He picked up one and tucked it in his pocket.

"Stop making so much noise," Jared said, trying to climb down carefully and nearly toppling a copper rosebush.

They knelt beside the glass case, and Jared unlatched it. There was a hiss as the lid lifted, as though some invisible gas was escaping. Inside, Mallory was motionless.

"Mallory," Jared said. "Get up." He pulled at her arm, but it was limp and flopped back onto her chest when he let go.

"You don't think someone needs to kiss her, do you?" Simon asked. "Like Snow White?"

"That's gross." Jared couldn't remember anything about kissing in the field guide, but he couldn't remember anything about glass coffins, either. He leaned in and gave her a quick peck on the cheek. There was no response.

"We have to do something," Simon said. "We don't have much time."

Jared grabbed a lock of Mallory's hair and tugged hard. She twitched slightly and half opened her eyes. Jared sighed with relief.

"Getoffme," she muttered, and tried to turn on her side.

"Help me get her up," Jared said, moving the sword off her and onto the floor.

He pulled her body a little ways up before she slipped back into the case.

"Come on, Mal," Jared said into her ear. *"Up!"*

Simon slapped her cheek. She twitched again, opening her eyes groggily.

"Wha—," she managed.

"You have to get out of there," said Simon. "Stand up."

"Lean on the sword like a cane," Jared suggested.

With her brothers' help Mallory managed to get on her feet and stagger out into the hallway. It was empty.

"Lean on the sword like a cane."

"For once," Simon said, "things are actually going our way."

Just then they heard the distant sound of hollow, metallic barking.

"The stones. The stones speak. They speak to me."

Chapter Six

IN WHICH the Stones Speak

Jared and Simon ran, half dragging Mallory, through a series of hallways and narrow, dim rooms. Once, they passed through an overhang high above a central cavity where the Korting oversaw dwarves laboring to stack weapons onto carts. The barking, at first far off, became closer and more frenzied. They continued on, through chamber after chamber, ducking behind stalagmites when they heard dwarves nearby, and then creeping on.

Jared stopped in a cavern with pools where white, sightless fish darted. Tiny rocks were balanced atop the points of all the stalagmites, and the sound of water droplets echoed through the space, along with a strange tapping rhythm. "Where are we?"

"I'm not sure," Simon said. "I would have remembered those fish, but I don't. I don't think we came this way when they brought us in."

"Where are we?" Mallory moaned, swaying slightly as she stood.

"We can't go back," Jared said nervously. "We have to keep going."

A small, pale figure jumped out from the shadows. It had huge, luminous eyes that shone in the gloom. On its forehead, two long whiskers quivered.

"Wha—what's that?" Simon whispered.

The creature tapped on the wall with one long, multijointed finger, then pressed a large ear against the stone. Jared noticed that the creature's nails were cracked and broken.

"Thestones. Thestonesspeak. Theyspeaktome." It had a small, whispery voice, and Jared strained to pick out individual words. The creature tapped again. The sound was like some demented Morse code.

"Hey," Jared said. "Um, do you know the way out of here?"

"Shhhhh." It closed its eyes and nodded its head in time with something Jared couldn't hear. Then it leaped into Jared's arms, wrapping

a strong hand around his neck. Jared stumbled backward.

"Yes! Yes! Thestonessaytocrawlthroughthere." It pointed into the darkness, past the pools of white fish.

"Um, great. Thanks." Jared tried to peel the creature off. Finally it unlatched, scrambled to the wall, and began tapping again.

"What is that?" Simon whispered to Jared. "A really weird dwarf?"

"A nodder or a banger, I think," Jared whispered back. "They live in mines and warn miners of collapses and stuff."

Simon made a face. "Are they all insane? It's worse than that phooka."

"Foryou,JaredGrace." The creature pressed a smooth, cold stone into Jared's hand. *"Thestonewantstotravelwithyou."*

"Uh, thanks," Jared said. "We have to go

"The stones speak."

now." He moved toward the dark place that the nodder-banger-thing had indicated. As Jared got closer, he thought he could make out a crevice.

"Wait. How did you know Jared's name?" Mallory asked, moving slowly behind her brothers.

Jared turned back, suddenly confused. "Yeah, how *did* you know my name?" he demanded.

The creature rapped on the cave wall again, an uneven series of taps. *"Thestonestellme. Thestonesknowall."*

"Riiiight." Jared continued on. The creature had actually pointed them toward a small opening in the wall of the cave. They had overlooked it before. The hole was low to the ground and very dark. Jared got on his hands and knees and started to crawl. The cave floor was moist, and sometimes he thought he could hear a slither or a rustle just ahead of him. His brother and sister shuffled along behind. Once or twice he heard one of them gasp, but he didn't slow his pace. He could still hear the barking of the dogs echoing through the caverns.

They emerged in the hall of the ironwood tree.

"I think it's that way," Jared said, pointing to one of the hallways.

They ran down the path until they came to a long fissure, almost as wide as Jared was tall. He looked down into the darkness. It was as black as if the crack went on forever.

"We have to jump!" Simon said. "Come on!"

"What?" said Mallory.

The barking was close behind them. Jared

Together they leaped.

saw red eyes in the gloom. Simon stepped back, then sprung across, landing hard.

"You have to!" Jared said, and grabbed hold of his sister's hand. Together they leaped. Mallory stumbled when her foot hit the rock on the other side, but she fell safely onto the cave floor. They sprinted off, hoping the dogs could not jump as far as they had.

But this passage circled around, and they found themselves back in the central hall, massive branches hanging above them, metal birds twittering.

"Where are we going?" Mallory whined as she leaned on the sword.

"I don't know," Jared said, catching his breath. "I don't know! I don't know!"

"I think maybe that way," Simon offered.

"We already went that way, and we wound up here!" The barking of the dogs was so close that Jared expected them to burst into the room at any moment.

"How can you not know where to go?" Mallory demanded. "Do you remember how you got in here?"

"I'm trying! It was dark, and we were in a cage! What do you want me to do?" Jared kicked the base of the tree as if to emphasize his point.

The leaves quivered, clanging together like a thousand chimes. The sound was deafening. One of the copper birds fell to the ground, its wings still twitching and its beak opening and closing soundlessly.

"Oh, crap," said Mallory.

Metal dogs burst into the room from several corridors, their sleek, jointed bodies effortlessly covering the distance between the entrance and the siblings. Their garnet eyes blazed.

"Climb!" Jared yelled, hooking his foot on

Metal dogs burst into the room.

the lowest branch and reaching back for his sister's hand. Simon clamored up the rough iron bark. Mallory lifted herself dazedly.

"Come on, Mallory!" Simon pleaded.

She swung her leg onto a branch just as a dog lunged. Its teeth caught hold of the end of her white dress and ripped it. The other dogs swarmed close, tearing the cloth.

Jared threw the stone that he'd been clutching in one hand. It flew past the dog's head and rolled ineffectually against the cave wall.

One of the dogs bounded after the rock. At first Jared thought that maybe the stone was magical. Then he noticed that the dog had carried it back in its teeth, metal tail wagging like a whip.

"Simon," Jared said. "I think that dog is *playing*."

Simon looked at the dog for a moment and then started to shimmy down the tree.

"What are you doing?" Mallory demanded. "Mechanical robot dogs are not pets!"

"Don't worry," Simon called back.

Simon dropped to the ground, and the dogs stopped barking suddenly, nosing him as though

deciding whether or not to bite. Simon stood very still. Watching him, Jared couldn't breathe.

"Good boys," Simon soothed, his voice shaking only slightly. "Want to fetch? Want to play a game?" He reached forward and gingerly took the stone from between the dog's metal teeth.

All the dogs bounced in the air at once, barking happily. Simon looked up at his siblings and smiled.

"You have got to be kidding me," Mallory said.

Simon threw the stone, and all five dogs bounded after it. One snatched it up in its jaws and marched back proudly, the others trailing eagerly. Simon leaned down to pet their metal heads. Their silver tongues lolled from their mouths.

Simon threw the rock three more times before Jared called down to him.

"We have to go," he said. "The dwarves are

going to find us if we wait any longer."

Simon looked disappointed. "Okay," he shouted to them. Then he took the stone and hurled it as hard as he could into the other room. The dogs thundered after it. "Come on!"

Jared and Mallory jumped down. All three of them ran to the small crack in the wall and squeezed inside, crawling rapidly on their hands and knees. Jared stuffed his backpack behind him, blocking the way. Already he could hear the dogs whining and scratching at the cloth.

They felt their way in the dark, but there must have been a fork in the tunnel that they'd missed earlier, because this time there was a soft, warm light at the end of the corridor.

They found themselves standing above the quarry on dewy grass. Dawn reddened the sky in the east.

"What happened?"

Chapter Seven

IN WHICH There Is an Unexpected Betrayal

Mallory looked down at herself in disgust. "I *hate* dresses. What happened? Why did I wake up in a glass box?"

Jared shook his head. "We're not really sure—I guess the dwarves grabbed you somehow. Do you remember anything?"

"I was packing up my things after the match." She shrugged. "Some kid said that you were in trouble."

"Shhh," Simon said, pointing into the quarry. "Get down."

They knelt in the grass and peered over the

edge. A horde of goblins poured out of the caves.
They skittered and rolled, gnashing their teeth
and barking before fanning out and sniffing the
air. Behind them was a massive monster with
dead branches for hair. It wore the dark, tattered
remains of clothes from another time, and big,
curving horns rose up from his brow.

From the cave entrance the Korting and his
dwarven courtiers appeared. Behind them
came more goblins, who were pulling a cart
filled with shining weapons. With that last group
a prisoner stumbled along ahead of them. The
prisoner was the size of an adult human, a sack
covering the person's head, both wrists and
ankles bound with dirty cloth. Something
about the person seemed familiar. The
goblins pushed the prisoner out into

the quarry, poking the figure with sharp sticks, far from where the monster stood.

"Who is that?" Mallory whispered, squinting.

"I can't see," said Jared. "Why would they need a prisoner?"

The Korting cleared his throat nervously as a hush fell over the crowd. "Great Lord Mulgarath, we thank you for the honor of allowing us to serve you."

Mulgarath stopped. The ogre's great horned head loomed over the rest of the creatures as he turned back to the dwarves with a sneer.

Jared swallowed hard. *Mulgarath.* The word had never meant much to him before, but now he was afraid. Even though he knew the monster couldn't see him, he felt those dark eyes sweep over the throng and wanted to duck down lower.

"Are these all the weapons I asked for?" Mulgarath's ringing tones echoed through the quarry. He pointed to the cart.

"Yes, of course," said the dwarf lord. "A show of our loyalty, our dedication to your new regime. You will find no finer blades, no better craftsmanship. I would stake my life on it!"

"Would you?" asked the ogre. He drew Jared's fake field guide from a large pocket. "And this—would you also stake your life that this is the book I asked you to obtain?"

The dwarf lord hesitated. "I . . . I did as you asked. . . ."

The ogre held up a battered book with a laugh. Jared realized it was the same laugh that the Not-Jared had made in the hallway at school.

Jared gasped and Mallory elbowed him hard.

"You have been duped, dwarf lord. No matter. I have Arthur Spiderwick's Guide," Mulgarath said. "The final thing I need to begin my reign."

The dwarf bowed low. "You are great indeed," the Korting said. "A worthy master."

"I may be a worthy master, but I am not at all sure that you make worthy servants." He

"Kill them!"

raised his hand, and his goblins stopped their scuffling and scrabbling. "Kill them!"

It happened so fast that Jared couldn't follow it all. The goblins seemed to surge forth as one, some stopping to pick up the dwarf-forged weapons, most just attacking with their claws and teeth. The dwarves hesitated, shouting, and that moment of panic and confusion was enough for the goblins to be upon them.

The goblins bit, clawed, and slashed until not a single dwarf was left standing.

Jared felt sick and numb. He had never seen anything be killed before. Looking down, he felt like he might throw up. "We have to stop them."

"There's no way we can do this alone. Look at them all," Mallory said. Jared glanced at the sword still clutched in Mallory's hand, its fine blade gleaming in the rising sun. It would

never be enough to take on all of them.

"We *have* to tell Mom what's going on," Simon said.

"She won't believe us!" Jared said. He wiped the wetness from his eyes with his shirt sleeve and tried not to look down at the broken bodies in the quarry. "What if she doesn't believe us?"

"We have to try," said Mallory.

And so, with the screams of dwarves still echoing in their ears, the three Grace children started toward home.

End of

BOOK FOUR

About TONY DiTERLIZZI . . .

A *New York Times* best-selling author, Tony DiTerlizzi created the Zena Sutherland Award–winning *Ted, Jimmy Zangwow's Out-of-This-World Moon Pie Adventure*, as well as illustrations in Tony Johnston's Alien and Possum beginning-reader series. Most recently, his brilliantly cinematic version of Mary Howitt's classic *The Spider and the Fly* was awarded a Caldecott Honor. In addition, Tony's art has graced the work of such well-known fantasy names as J.R.R. Tolkien, Anne McCaffrey, Peter S. Beagle, and Greg Bear as well as Wizards of the Coast's *Magic The Gathering*. He and his wife, Angela, reside with their pug, Goblin, in Amherst, Massachusetts. Visit Tony on the World Wide Web at www.diterlizzi.com.

and HOLLY BLACK

An avid collector of rare folklore volumes, Holly Black spent her early years in a decaying Victorian mansion where her mother fed her a steady diet of ghost stories and books about faeries. Accordingly, her first novel, *Tithe: A Modern Faerie Tale,* is a gothic and artful glimpse at the world of Faerie. Published in the fall of 2002, it received two starred reviews and a Best Book for Young Adults citation from the American Library Association. She lives in West Long Branch, New Jersey, with her husband, Theo, and a remarkable menagerie. Visit Holly on the World Wide Web at www.blackholly.com.

Tony and Holly continue to work day and night fending off angry faeries and goblins in order to bring the Grace children's story to you.

Who has been captured?
Is the Guide gone?
Can three weary children
do it alone?

MULGARATH

Can they face an ogre
with an evil plan
to conquer the planet
and poison the land?

*Or is there someone
brave, strong, and wise
who can battle a monster
and come out alive?*

?

*Where is our hero?
Seek Spiderwick five.*

THE WRATH OF MULCARATH
BOOK FIVE OF FIVE

ACKNOWLEDGMENTS

Tony and Holly would like to thank
Steve and Dianna for their insight,
Starr for her honesty,
Josh and Lisa for their attention to detail,
Myles and Liza for sharing the journey,
Ellen and Julie for helping make this our reality,
Kevin for his tireless enthusiasm and faith in us,
and especially Angela and Theo—
there are not enough superlatives
to describe your patience
in enduring endless nights
of Spiderwick discussion.

The text type for this book is set in Cochin.
The display types are set in Nevins Hand and Rackham.
The illustrations are rendered in pen and ink.
Production editor: Dorothy Gribbin
Art director: Dan Potash
Production managers: Chava Wolin and Karene Petrillo